I0530902

Breaking Free

The Story of Independence and Self-Discovery…

Elle Lanelle

For more information or details on this publication please address Maine
& Moss, customerservice@maineandmoss.com.

Library of Congress Control Number: XXXXXXXXXX
ISBN-10: 0989127206
ISBN-13: 978-0-9891272-0-2

Printed in the United States of America
10 9 8   7 6 5 4 3 2   1

Breaking Free – first paperback

E-mail: terianelle@gmail.com
www.facebook.com/terianelle

Formatting / Editing / Cover Artwork by: Maine & Moss

ACKNOWLEDGEMENTS

Elle Lanelle would like to thank all the authors before her, for their great works and inspiration. Also, her publisher and supporter who has guided her each step of the way. And her family for their constant support. Much love to them all.

Breaking Free

Elle Lanelle

Princess

Captured…

Not too many people in the world can say they are a Princess. Most Princesses come about because they were born or married into a regal family. Therefore, it is implied that they must also acquire a great deal of wealth. But I know a Princess who was neither born nor married into a regal family nor has she acquired any amount of wealth. In fact, she can be described as average.

As a young Princess, everything was handed to her without her doing much asking. When she did ask, it was given her as well. Nothing was ever denied her. Even if Mom or Dad said that they might not get it for her, the next thing she knew she was playing with the very thing she asked for. Wasn't she such a blessed child?

As she reached into her older years, more was expected of her - as to be expected as a part of life. She was expected to do more chores and to show insight that she was maturing. Well, if she wasn't a Princess she may have been expected to show more maturity. However, Dad was just fine with his daughter remaining as his Little Princess and Mom didn't say anything about it either. So she guessed they were happy that she, as their Princess, remained the same.

When a chore was assigned to her, it usually got done and was done in the way that was expected. But there were times when, whether purposely or not, one or more chores would not get done. And neither Mom nor Dad would say much about it. They may question and then tell Princess to do it but wouldn't make a big deal out of it. And usually Princess would do it but if she didn't, nothing much would be said. There was barely any penalty.

Now this had been going on for years and Princess has

reached her late teens. By this age, most children have acquired a certain set of domestic skills: cleaning, washing, cooking, basic sewing, basic hair, and the like. But Princess is not like other children. The only things she can do are clean and wash. Well, she can iron too but she really tries to avoid that as much as possible. Most children (or people) wash clothes weekly or twice a month or even monthly, but not Princess. She'll have clothes in the hamper for months or until she runs out of undergarments, whichever is the longest period of time. And if no one asks her to clean, she won't do it. But she has no problem keeping her own body clean. She can stay in a tub or shower for 30mins or more. It drives her family crazy but she takes that much time anyway. Oh well. . .

As Princess got older, tensions arose between her and her parents. But that is no surprise to the general public. There have been times when Princess and her parents have argued.

And they have said many things to her such as: "If you keep this up, I'll send you away so you straighten up your act." "If you don't like it here, you can live somewhere else." "Your life? You have no life. Your life is out on the streets." Now such comments may seem harsh to some but not to Princess. At first, she was scared of these threats and would start to behave. But after a while, she was back to disobeying and threats were made again. This was repeated throughout Princess's early teenage years. But after some time, Princess noticed (first subconsciously) that these threats were just like balloons – full of hot air. They possessed no substance, no weight and therefore had very little effect on Princess's behavior.

So whenever Princess's parents got on her about this and that, she virtually ignored them. It meant nothing to her on what they were saying. Granted, they would be talking about important life lessons but Princess could find no actual value in what they were saying. "And why is that?" you may ask. Because Princess lived a very comfortable life. The hardships and pressures of the world had little to no effect on her because Mom and Dad took care of everything. Princess was as comfortable as a 40-year-old man living with his mom. Excuse the stereotypical cliché.

She has been so comfortable that she barely has a social life. Princess has only one friend, Amiga. And Amiga's home life is like the polar opposite to that of Princess's. They have both physical and personality similarities but once you start talking about living in each of their houses, they are as different as Night and Day. Princess knows about the home life of Amiga and sometimes it can be quite sad. But other times, Princess feels jealous of Amiga.

"Why" you say "when she has the most comfortable life anyone can ever have?" Because Princess has realized that having such a comfortable life has actually greatly impaired her. Princess is convinced that if someone left her in the world, to fend for herself, she would die within three months; whereas Amiga would begin to thrive after six months.

Because her parents have always given her things without her having to work for them, Princess goes around hoping that the world or people in the world will basically give her free handouts without effort from her. Because Princess rarely answered for her disobedience (or wasn't punished enough), she kind of goes around feeling that she can get away with anything. She doesn't fully understand the consequences of her actions so she does them anyway. It's a very dangerous way to be but it is what she is used to.

And she is very much aware of this. She knows she should try to have a better attitude about things and better herself, but she finds it very difficult to change herself and her attitude. So it looks like Princess's next option is to get help so that her attitude can change. But Princess feels she is better off keeping her feelings to herself.

When she has tried to explain to her parents how she is feeling about something, Princess usually just ends up feeling worse than she did before she said anything. And no one seems to understand where she is coming from or how she feels. To them, she is just an overemotional, hormonal, PMSing teenager whose emotions and feelings are run by whether she is on her period or not.

This saddens Princess very much and makes her feel alone in the world. Princess doesn't even feel that Amiga truly understands or even tries to understand. If Princess appears to be overly emotional, Amiga will say that it must be almost "that time of the month." Princess hates to hear this because that's not the case. Princess is just having an internal turmoil that no one is willing to understand. If Amiga is having some kind of breakdown, everyone understands and is completely sympathetic. But let Princess have the same kind of breakdown and everyone just assumes her menstrual is coming or she is just overreacting to something. Apparently, her emotions don't matter much and are over exaggerated. Sigh...

What will Princess do about the situation she is in? How will she overcome it? Who knows? But whatever happens, Princess better do something quick before the effects are irreversible....

Rebel

Trapped…

When people hear the word rebel or think of a rebellion, it usually has a negative connotation to it. But there are some instances when people will look at a rebellion as a benefit, even valuable to society. But what about someone who seems to rebel against life itself? Is that person of benefit to society? Is that person valuable?

Rebel is a girl I know. She lives with her parents and attends college. Her parents pay her bills, including cell phone which she uses a lot to text her friends. And they provide her with money to get back and forth to school. She has no job but why would she need one when her parents pay for everything? She has a pretty comfortable life for she was raised as a Princess.

Rebel has been pretty happy with this life she lives. But lately she has been doing a lot of questioning, especially when it comes to school and her future. For some time she's been pursuing a major, but lately... she's been questioning about whether or not she wants to continue to do it. Plus, others have told her that she may not have the personality for it. When the subject of pursuing a different career came up, Mom became quite defensive and said things like "Why do you want to change now all of a sudden? Are the classes you already took going to even count for a different major? Is it going to make you stay in school longer? I don't like to spend money where I feel it will be wasted. I don't like wasting money." Funny, I never knew that paying for your child's education counted as a waste of money. But of course, Rebel never once said that she was actually going to change majors. It was just a thought in her head, an idea.

But, as always, a simple statement of hers is taken all out of proportion without any further explanation from her. She's sure that this happens because it's actually an original thought of her own. See what happened was that Rebel was pretty much forced to go to college. Ever since she was born, Dad has always said "You're going to college." And there was no arguing. But then again, why would a 5-year-old argue with her father? So her future was predetermined for her. And, of course, she went unprepared especially since the media makes a joke, downgrades, and over exaggerates life, particularly those of adolescence and in college. So she went to college unprepared and predisposition. And of course, Mom and Dad paid for everything.

At first, there was no problem with Mom and Dad paying for everything. Their only rule was that Rebel attends her classes and get at least Bs in them. Sure, every so often, they would tell Rebel that she needed to look for scholarships to help pay for school. But, of course, Rebel didn't do as she was told and therefore her parents had to pay for everything out of pocket (Rebel's been denied State and Federal Aid). And her parents said absolutely nothing about it. I mean, yea they would complain for a time that Rebel needed to look for scholarships but they never stopped paying for her to go to school. Maybe if they did stop paying, Rebel would have seen the importance of looking for scholarships and therefore be able to take responsibility for her own education. But now, Rebel is starting to have a different outlook on things.

Rebel has had enough of being treated like a Princess and she is ready to take a stand. She's realized that the way her parents pamper her have actually inhibited her from making responsible decisions like a mature individual. So she has developed a game plan and this plan basically involves her not telling her parents about what she is up to. She will just do things and hope for the best. Besides, why should she tell her parents when all they are going to say is that it's about time she did something with her life, it's about time she got things done and started acting like an adult? And they will probably comment on the fact that she has the pattern of not following things through. So why go through the headache of hearing her parents say things like that? Rebel needs encouragement and not to be berated. She also doesn't need the tone her parents like to use with her.

For her game plan, Rebel has decided to start by looking for a job. She refuses to tell her parents of any interviews she goes on. She'll tell them about the job once she gets it. If they ask her about any interviews she went on, then she will tell them about it but not before. If they ask her about her decision to work at a certain place, she will tell them that she wants to gain a wide range of experience and be exposed to different types of jobs and businesses. She really looks forward to their reactions hehe.

After she gets her job, she plans to save up at least half of each paycheck if possible. She's sure that her parents will ask her how much money she'll be making. She's debating on whether or not to tell them the full amount. She doesn't want to be mooched off of but she also wants to assist her family financially. However, she doesn't want them to ask all the time. After all, she does want to save up her money for things she wants and needs. The whole point of her finding a job is so that she can take care of herself so her parents don't have to anymore (and to pay off increasing debts). I guess in her mind she is just trying to become an independent young woman.

Concerning school, she will start applying for scholarships. She hopes she will get enough to be able to pay for her entire time in school. At first, Rebel will say nothing about the scholarships. But when Mom starts asking about her school bill, then Rebel will tell them that she has received scholarships. Of course, they will wonder why she didn't say anything before. Rebel will probably just say something along the lines of "not sure if I was even going to win them" or "not sure when they were going to take effect." This will probably cause Mom to comment on Rebel's initiative but also her secretiveness, which Mom is beginning to get fed up about. And still another option is that Mom (or even Dad) will say something like "It's about time you went out and applied for scholarships." Part of me thinks that Rebel wants a negative reaction from her parents. I don't know why she would want that though (shrug).

When all of that is taken cared of, Rebel will be saving up so she can get an apartment. Hopefully, Amiga will also have a job and be able to save up. That way they will be able to get an apartment together and move out of their crazy homes. Both of them need a change of scenery and just need to get out before they go permanently insane. It's so weird how much their lives parallel each other. Rebel thinks that's what makes them such great friends.

Will Rebel be able to carry out her plans? Will she find her independence? If she does, will she be able to adjust and like it? Will Rebel find her peace of mind and happiness in this world? Will she be able to break free?

Birdie

Liberated…

Have you ever looked up at the sky at the birds as they fly by? Have you ever watched as a bird pecks along the ground? Have you ever thought to yourself about how free the birds are? How they appear to go through life without a care in the world? Have you ever thought of what it would be like to live life with the attitude of a bird? Well, I know someone who has accomplished this to a degree.

Her name is Birdie and she is not wealthy nor incredibly intelligent by any standard. She is not immune to the pains and distresses of being a human born into this world. She must still take care of her health and she must still purchase different products and services that this world has to offer. All in all, she must and does live in this world like you and I. She does not live in a fantasy world and is not admitted into an asylum. "Well then how," you may ask, "can she be so carefree like the birds when she faces the same problems as we do?" The answer, my friends, is something quite simple and not incredibly difficult to obtain. My friends, she is satisfied and happy with her life. "How can that be?"

Well, Birdie has learned to be content with what she has. This contentment she has was found in pursuing spiritual things. She found the real truth about God and never let it go. She allows the Bible and the standards and principles found within to permeate throughout every aspect of her life. And thanks to Bible principles, she has learned how to be happy with life despite the hardships it includes.

Two Bible principles that have become the theme of her life are found at Matthew chapter 6 verse 22, which talks about having a 'simple eye,' and First Timothy chapter 6 verse 8, which speaks about being content with "sustenance and covering." With just these two principles first, Birdie was able to shape her entire life. She molded her life in line with the Scriptures. And this has caused her to be content with the things she possesses. She finds that it relieves a great deal of stress.

She has her own place, which she shares with Amiga. They've been roomies for a while and it has worked out well. And the apartment is not too expensive for them to afford. In short, they have the bare minimal that they need to live; nothing more, nothing extravagant, just a basic apartment for two separate females who obviously need their own space.

Birdie also has a job. However, her job is freelancing and therefore she has her good months and her bad months. But she's never needed to find a "regular" job. She considers this to be a blessing. If she is a bit short on funds, she goes to work for her publisher temporarily. Sometimes she'll work for her publisher even during a good month. She likes her publisher I guess.

However, not everyone is happy with the decision she made regarding her career choice. The main ones who are not happy are Mom and Dad. Oddly enough, they are unhappy for fairly different reasons. Dad is not happy because he feels that if Birdie really wanted to freelance then she should have gotten started earlier instead of waiting to like "the last minute," in a way. Mom is mad because she feels Birdie wasted her time in school, getting a degree for a major that has nothing to do with freelancing. But what Mom fails to realize is that Birdie actually uses her major to freelance about it. Also, Mom feels that freelancing is not a "real" job. But with freelancing, Birdie is able to keep her mind focused on spiritual things.

Honestly, Mom isn't angry about Birdie's spiritual pursuits. Mom is just upset and worried that Birdie's freelancing won't be enough to support her in the long run. However, Mom fails to remember that with freelancing, Birdie is able to work from anywhere and freelancers will always be useful. Plus, Birdie knows that if she relies on God that He will always provide for her. Therefore, Birdie will always have a job and will be able to accomplish her goals. But even if she is out of work for a while, she knows that if she continues to focus on spiritual things, God will make a way for her to obtain a new job. So she isn't worried about that. That's one less stress in her life. Plus, freelancing is more than just a job for Birdie. Freelancing is actually her passion, her hobby, so work is never dull for her. Granted, she does experience some dry spells but for the most part, ideas are constantly flowing through her mind. She has so many that she barely has time to get them all down.

Basically, Birdie lives a simple life mostly only surviving on the bare minimal essentials. When funds prove available, she will treat herself and or Amiga to something that can be described as extra, a want, or a bit extravagant such as a day-long trip to a spa or a trip outside their state or even outside their region. But I'm not going to sit here and tell you that everything came easy to Birdie; that as soon as she decided to freelance, she made X amount of dollars and continued to make that much every month until she had what she needed to be on her own. No, I won't say that. For one, it would be a lie and two, it would be unrealistic.

Like I said before, Birdie faces the same problems and pressures of this world just like everyone else. She didn't just wake up one day, decide to freelance, and succeeded on her very first try. No, she had to work hard to make her first freelance project work in her benefit. And while she did so, she did have a "regular" job. It was tough and she found that she did not particularly enjoy it. It was neither her co-workers nor her workload that made her dislike her job; she just wasn't as passionate about it as she was when she first pursued the major for it.

And when she first moved out of her parents' home, she found living on her own (even with a roomie like Amiga) to be very challenging. Though she asked for advice and suggestions, nothing anyone said could have fully prepared her for the "culture shock" of moving out on her own. At times, it even proved to be scary for her. Several times, she has thought of going back home to her parents. She did only once temporarily when she was moving from one apartment to another. Other than that, she has been on her own, separate from her parents. It took her a while before she completely settled into her own place and adjusted to being on her own.

And when she did move out on her own, Mom and Dad were not particularly happy about it. They would have loved it if she had waited until later to move out. But Birdie figured it would be better for her to move sooner rather than later. Such a decision came with its own share of problems, both in her life and with her parents, but Birdie felt it was the right thing for her to do. After a while, Mom and Dad saw the benefit of Birdie making this decision and they helped to make the adjustment a little easier for her to handle. Not by providing anything or babying her, but by telling her what she needed to consider and by giving her tips on how to settle.

She did learn to settle and has loved her independence ever since. She also loves the life she lives, free of unnecessary stresses and manageable. She is well socially, mentally, physically, and, above all, spiritually. As she looks back on her life and decisions, does she regret any she has made? No, she does not. The only thing she might change is that she had realized the danger of her Princess childhood earlier, became a Rebel sooner, and broke free of her confinement. But, above all, she has no regrets.

The End

www.ingramcontent.com/pod-product-compliance
Lightning Source LLC
Chambersburg PA
CBHW071227130626
46555CB00004B/1876